E/T
T/T Titherington,
     Jeanne

     Pumpkin pumpkin

$11.88

DATE DUE

OCT 17 1995

NOV 23 1994

NOV 3 1994

OCT 27 1993

DEC 13 1993

APR 19 1993

Pumpkin
Pumpkin

by Jeanne Titherington

Greenwillow Books
New York

JAMIE'S SEEDS

WITH SPECIAL THANKS TO SAM

COLORED PENCILS WERE USED FOR THE FULL-
COLOR ART. THE TEXT TYPE IS ITC CASLON NO. 224
AND THE DISPLAY TYPE IS CASLON OPEN FACE.

LIBRARY OF CONGRESS CATALOGING IN PUBLICATION DATA

TITHERINGTON, JEANNE.
PUMPKIN PUMPKIN.
SUMMARY: JAMIE PLANTS A PUMPKIN SEED AND,
AFTER WATCHING IT GROW, CARVES IT, AND SAVES
SOME SEEDS TO PLANT IN THE SPRING.
1. CHILDREN'S STORIES, AMERICAN.
[1. PUMPKIN—FICTION.
2. GARDENING—FICTION] I. TITLE.
PZ7.T53PU 1985   [E]   84-25334
ISBN 0-688-05695-4
ISBN 0-688-05696-2 (LIB. BDG.)

FOR

JAMES AND THE FISH

amie planted
a pumpkin seed,

and the pumpkin seed
grew a pumpkin sprout,

and the pumpkin sprout
grew a pumpkin plant,

and the pumpkin plant
grew a pumpkin flower,

and the pumpkin flower
grew a pumpkin.

And the pumpkin grew…

and grew…

and grew,

until Jamie picked it.

Then Jamie scooped out
the pumpkin pulp,
carved a pumpkin face,
and put it in the window.
But…

he saved
six pumpkin seeds
for planting in the spring.